The Peddler's Bed

written by
Lauri Fortino

illustrated by
Bong Redila

Ripple Grove Press
Portland, OR

First Edition 2015
Library of Congress Control Number 2014957940
ISBN 978-0-9913866-3-5

2 4 6 8 10 9 7 5 3 1

Printed in South Korea by PACOM

This book was typeset in Alberta, Amigo, and Garamond.
The illustrations were rendered in watercolor and ink.
Book designed by Bong Redila

Ripple Grove Press
Portland, OR

Visit us at www.RippleGrovePress.com

To my family, especially my grandmother, Harriet Whipple, from whom I inherited the writer's gene.

—L. F.

To my wife, Arceli, and daughter, Oneng, thank you for letting me daydream all day. To my mom and dad for taking care of their kids. And to my grandparents for letting us stay in their old house every summer when we were kids.

—B. R.

One afternoon, a little man was working in his tiny garden
next to his small house when he heard *squeak, squeak, squeak.*

He saw a peddler driving his cart along the narrow road.
The little man's dog, Happy, barked a friendly greeting.

The peddler stopped his cart and
climbed down from his seat.
"It's a fine day," he said.

"Truly," answered the little man,
"and that's a fine bed you have there
in your cart."

"I crafted the bed from the hardy oak trees
that grow on the other side of the hills,"
said the peddler,
"and I filled the mattress with the
softest goose-down feathers."

"How wonderful," said the little man.

"The bed is so sturdy that I guarantee
it will never squeak," said the peddler.

"Never squeak," echoed the little man.
"All beds squeak a bit."

"Not this one. Let me show you."

The peddler slid his oak bed down onto the road.
Then he stepped on top of it and jumped up and down several times.
The fine, strong bed did not squeak, not once.

"That is a remarkable bed," said the little man.

"It's for sale," said the peddler, "at a very fair price."

"No doubt," said the little man,
"but I haven't even one penny to give you for it."

The peddler paused for a moment, and then he said, "I'll make
you a deal, sir. If you can think of a way to make my oak bed
squeak by sunset, it will be yours."

The little man's face lit up. "I have never owned such a fine bed
in all my life," he said. "Come, have a seat in the shade of my porch."

"Yes, thank you," answered the peddler.

The little man went into his house to fetch a cup.

Squeak, squeak, squeak, sounded the door
of the small, shabby house.

He went to his water pump.
Squeak, squeak, squeak, twanged the pump.

He filled the cup with cool water and
gave it to the peddler.

Then he filled a dimpled bucket
for the peddler's pony and a bowl
for Happy.

"Now, how shall I make the fine bed squeak?"
he thought aloud.

Happy chased a field mouse out of the garden.
Squeak, squeak, squeak, chirped the mouse.

"Hmm," uttered the little man.
He scooped the tiny mouse up and placed it upon the bed.

The bed was so snug that the
wee creature curled up and fell asleep.

"Oh well," said the little man
as he patted Happy's head.

"It's getting near suppertime,"
he said to the peddler.
"Do come in and have a bite to eat."

"I'd be delighted," answered the peddler.

"Have a seat at my table," said the little man.

Squeak, squeak, squeak, creaked the chair
as the peddler sat down.

"I'll fix us some soup," said the little man.

He went to his garden and dug up some potatoes,
carrots, and onions. He gave some of the carrots to
the peddler's pony. He returned to his house.

The little man made a fire. He hung a pail of water above it. He cut up the vegetables and dropped them into the pail. *Squeak, squeak, squeak,* chimed the pail as it swung above the fire.

He unwrapped a few scraps of meat. He cut a piece for Happy and put the rest into the pail. Before long, the soup was ready. The little man pressed his hands together and gave thanks for all that he had and for his good company.

"The day is nearly over and I can't think of any way to make your remarkable bed squeak," he said to the peddler.

"Ah," answered the peddler, "it's no use. My fine, sturdy bed will never squeak."

"Nonetheless," said the little man, "Happy and I are glad to have your company."

"And I'm grateful for your warm welcome," answered the peddler.
The peddler looked around the humble, one-room house. The little man's bed was nothing more than a pile of frayed, moth-eaten blankets in a corner near the fireplace.

"It will be dark soon," he said, "and I must get back on the road.
Would you like to sit on my fine bed before I go?"

"I would very much," answered the little man.

Squeak, squeak, squeak, sounded the door of the small, shabby house
as the peddler and the little man headed outside.

"It's a fine evening," said the little man.

"Yes, indeed," answered the peddler.

The little man sat upon the edge of the fine, oak bed.

"I would like to lie down for just a moment," he said.

Soon the little man was asleep.

Squeak, squeak, squeak, sang his nose as he breathed.

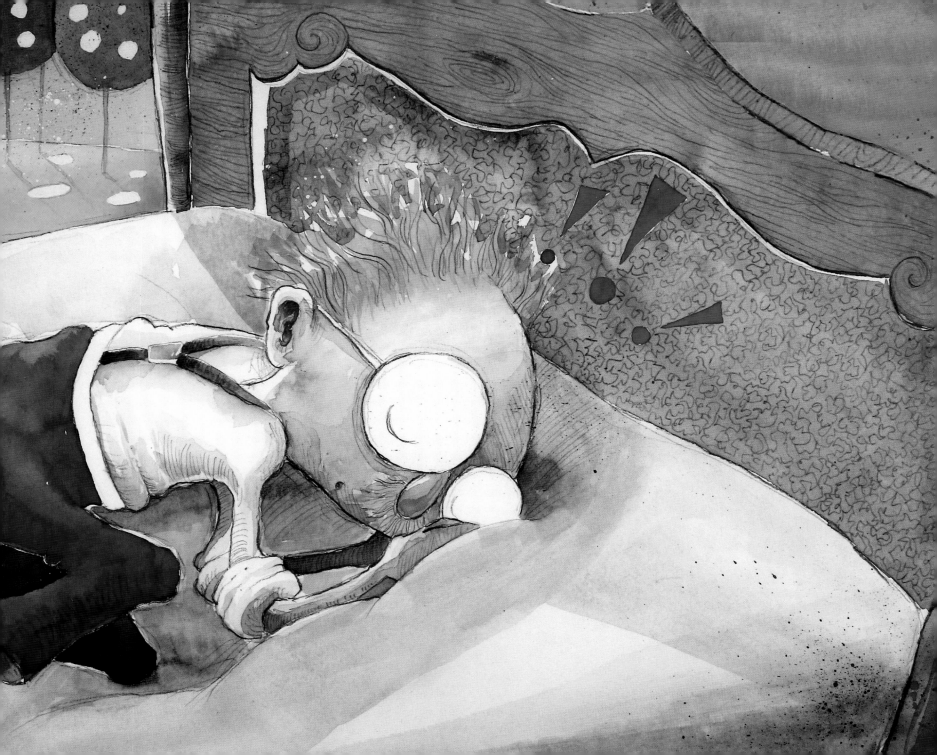

The peddler smiled as he carefully pushed the bed, with the little man upon it, onto the porch of the small, shabby house.

But the little man did not stir, for he was in a deep sleep.

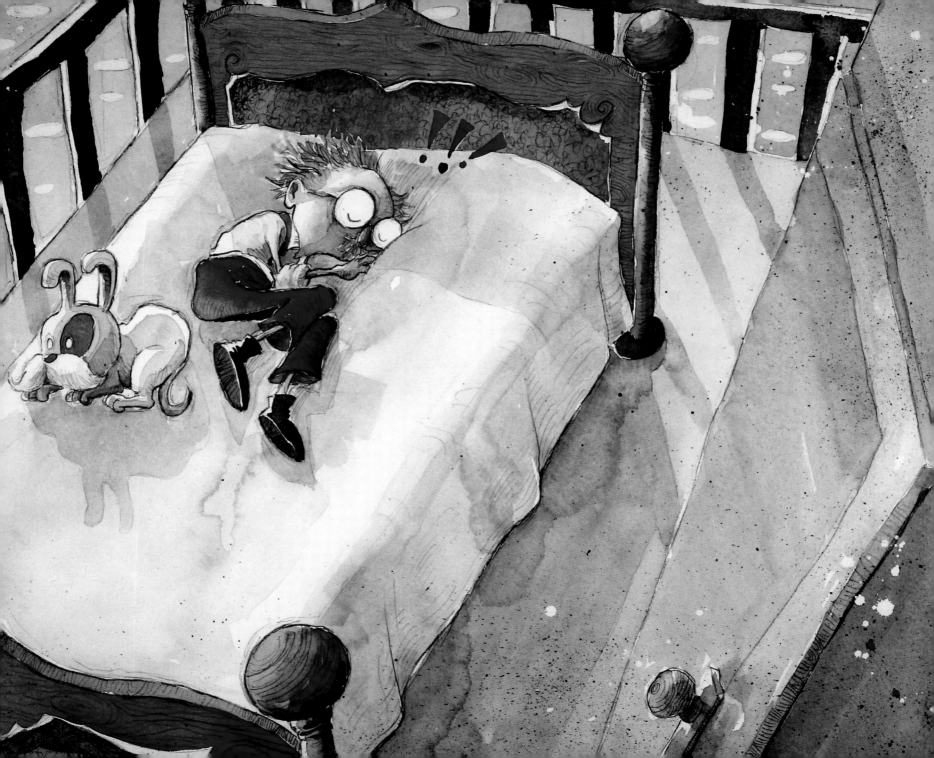

The peddler patted Happy on the head and then climbed into his cart.

He clucked to his pony and started off down the narrow road.
Squeak, squeak, squeak, sang the little man's nose as he slept.

Squeak, squeak, squeak,
echoed the wheels on the peddler's cart
as it disappeared around the bend.